SERGE FAUCHEREAU COMPLETE FIC

TION

TRANSLATED BY
RON PADGETT
AND JOHN ASHBERY
BLACK SQUARE EDITIONS
NEW YORK 2002

Copyright © 2002 by Serge Fauchereau | ISBN 0-9675144-8-7

Translation copyright © 2002 by Ron Padgett | Translation copyright © 2002 by John Ashbery | Some of these pieces are included in the following collections: *Fiction Complète* (Seghers, 1983); *Expositions et Affabulations* (Cercle d'Art, 1992); *Textes 1992–2002* (André Dimanche, 2003). | Many thanks to the editors of *Agni*, *Scarlet*, *New American Writing*, and *Série d'Ecriture*, in which some of these pieces originally appeared in translation. | This work, published as part of a program of aid for publication, received support from the French Ministry of Foreign Affairs and the Cultural Services of the French Embassy in the United States (www.frenchculture.org). | Black Square Editions is a wholly owned imprint of Hammer Books, a tax exempt (501c3), non-profit organization, and is distributed by Small Press Distribution, 1341 Seventh Street, Berkeley, CA 94710 Designed by Quemadura | Printed in Canada by Kromar Printing Ltd.

BLACK SQUARE EDITIONS | 1200 Broadway 3-c, New York, NY 10001

CONTENTS

from
COMPLETE FICTION
3

from
DISPLACEMENTS
57

from
DEMONSTRATIONS AND FABULATIONS
79

Ah, the horrible temptation to know everything that is found in books when one is also a bibliophobe totally in love with what happens in real life.

PIERRE REVERDY *En vrac*

> Ein Zeichen sind wir, deutunglos
> Schmerzlos sind wir und haben fast
> Die Sprache in der Fremde verloren.

FRIEDRICH HÖLDERLIN *Mnemosyne*

FROM

COMPLETE FICTION

TRANSLATED BY RON PADGETT

3

Thus always pushed, the lighter buildings have disappeared, the palaces have collapsed, their walls split open. There exists no dimension other than time, but time in your westernized cities treats you worse than the jungle that has devoured the buildings around here, because there still remain some traces of these bronze-skinned men, although the wind passing through the crests of the temples produces no sound and the dignitaries disappear as the stucco flakes off.

You, your enthusiasm, or your pain will be completely lost. Why cross the sea and travel across continents? You glance casually through the porthole at the stretches of water going by and you drink cocktails, you travel at night with your arms around someone who sleeps like a child. You don't want to think that time is following its own course at the same speed that neither drink nor the scent of hair could change, and the only thing you think about is seat reservations or how plastic upholstery causes sweating. Forgetful and frivolous, you don't really see the bluebonnets you pick in Buda, you don't really look at the station worker who argues with you in Vera Cruz, you hardly look at the subway passengers in Montreal, the canals in Amsterdam, the gables of Brussels. . . . Do we look enough at what we'll never see twice?

Space is imaginary. Only time exists, and time has no edges. Blond foreigners will come to sit in the shadow of the tower at Palenque. They will look at the big courtyard framed with staircases and they will take a few photographs of the nine stone giants, but nothing of their happiness will remain in this place, or else it will be like the inscriptions on the steps here, glyphs whose meaning no one understands.

5

An anonymous work of the fifteenth century, "Chevy Chase" is the most famous of the border ballads: several dozen quatrains divided into two fits. "Chevy Chase"—also a ragtime song that the pianist Eubie Blake composed in 1914. I heard it for the first time when the old man talked, on a television show, about his life. Also, there was a time when I parked my car at the Chevy Chase Residence. (Maybe it was called that because of the nearby Chevy Chase National Bank.) One night, making too fast a turn into the small parking lot, I had banged into and dented the rear bumper of this guy's Chevrolet. He wouldn't let me make reparation; he said it didn't matter. He just left the bumper dented. I never saw that mark on his car without feeling guilty. I saw him pretty often and, especially if he was with a relative or his friend (a mild-mannered fat guy), he never failed to greet me with some gibe like "Keep you spurs off the horsepower!" What could I say? I felt so alone facing their smiles. Every time I drove in or left, I saw that mark on his bumper, and it was as if I heard a metallic sound. I was mad at myself, I was mad at him. I told myself that one day I'd like to bash in his whole car, so as to be free of the inferior position he had forced me into.

If I go back to Lord Percy, he had said that he'd go hunting on Earl Douglas's land; and it was at dawn of a Monday that he set out for the hills with fifteen hundred archers, all bold of blood and bone. By noon, a hundred fat harts could be seen lying slain near the River Tweed. And then arrived Earl Douglas and the men of his clan, with lance, axe, and sword; hardier men of hand and heart there never were in Christendom. Who are ye, ye who arrogate the right to hunt in Chevy Chase? We will tell thee not, and hunt where we wish, in spite of thine and thee. The two armies clashed. Brandished swords, crests in the wind, crash of lances and bucklers. The river was deep and the middle of its bed was all sound and fury, with the clashing of arms, blood, and horses disemboweled. Douglas fell dead, a long arrow piercing lung and liver. Percy was run clean through with Montgomery's lance, who in turn received an arrow in the heart. They say that of the three thousand combattants, one hundred twenty-eight came through. The soldiers' bodies were mixed with the dead animals they thought they had fought over, at Chevy Chase.

Stories, like history, hardly vary. A slight change of period and frontier make it for rustling horses. O.K., here it is: the doctor and the three Earp Brothers have gone back up Fremont Street to confront two of the Clantons and Frank and Tom McLaury. These last two didn't have a chance: the first was shot down with a .45 slug in the belly, the second riddled by the doctor's buckshot. Young Clanton, hit several times, died less than a minute after this brief fusillade; at the first shot, his brother had ducked into the nearby photographer's shop. Apparently the opposing camp fared better: the oldest Earp got hit in the calf and the youngest in the right shoulder and back, though a few months later bushwackers would get them. The doctor, he would die of tuberculosis five years later. The middle Earp would live on for almost another half century.

I would know how to get back to Chevy Chase. After all these years, I remember its red and white houses. I'd turn on the radio full blast—maybe "Chevy Chase" would be on. Then the first left on the ring road, then the first right and, after the bank, another right. I've forgotten the streets' names but I still have the feel in my hands, and that old instinct would tell me, better than any sign, where to turn or to slow down.... 1388 or 1883, 1973 or 2036, stories, histories, it doesn't matter: its revolving light vanished, the police car that just went by, after a speeder—Chevy Chase?—has no more reality than a canvas painted a century earlier, some "Remise de chevreuils" ("Deer Shelter") by Courbet. Today, the old musician is as dead as Earl Douglas and Billy Clanton; that guy's Chevrolet must have been compacted, and people I don't know have taken our parking spaces in the Chevy Chase lot. I have no reason to go there anymore. The old story won't begin again. Valiant Percy and the doctor with the deadly shotgun—their vendettas merely brought them closer to their own deaths. For us, a car wreck will be good enough. The old story won't begin again. Who knows if the red and white houses have been torn down? The shape of a town changes quicker, alas, than a mortal's fear. Everything goes so fast. I'll never go back to Chevy Chase.

Of course it is useless to wish to be free of it: all those stories, all that music, all that art, the whole educational and cultural bazaar. We have been fed it so much and for so long that we have developed a dependence on it. It's hard to say whether it civilizes or paralyzes, but there's no escaping it. It's perhaps the only drug we never kick.

First, don't put your fingers in your nose, the official Residence and over there the Hassan Tower, "Frère Jacques," the blue trees are cedars and the white animals are sheep, borage is good for a fever. There's also the story of the wild swans: an evil queen gives the eleven princes and their sister Elisa only some bowls of sand to eat. One day, she changes the princes into wild swans and smears the princess with walnut stain. To release her brothers, Elisa has to gather nettles from the cemetery and weave them into boats that will change them back into men. Condemned to be burned at the stake as a witch, she just has time to throw the nettle coats onto the swans, who immediately turn into princes again. The youngest prince ends up with a swan's wing instead of an arm because Elisa hadn't been able to finish the last sleeve in time. But everyone is very happy anyway.

A lot of things will be piled onto these swans. Later "La Toilette d'Esther" by Chassériau, you never put your hand out first when shaking hands with a lady, bear stew in Warsaw, Marx and Bakunin in ..., "around the world." And then the Scottish poetry of the fifteenth century: Cressida is a coquette who quickly forgot, in the arms of other men, the tenderness of Troilus the knight: Fy on all suich! Fy on thaire doubilnesse! / Fy on thaire lust and bestly appetite! And if the others grow weary of her, Cressida does nothing but weep and implore Venus, to the point that her fickleness makes the gods indignant. Saturn takes away her beauty and Diana strikes her with leprosy. Repulsive, putrescent, and soon blind, Cressida is reduced to begging outside the town walls with the other lepers. One day, Troilus goes by with his splendid retinue. Troubled by the sight of that poor wretch, whom he doesn't recognize, he gives her alms and goes on, while she overhears the other lepers saying the name of the generous cavalier.

There are examples more cogent than a medieval poem or a fairy tale. It depends on each person and under what circumstances we learned about it—an understanding that henceforth will be within us, merely waiting for a signal to burst forth, with or against our will: a word, a gesture, a sound, a color.... Look: here's a couple strolling along a tree-lined walk in a park. You could linger over the young lady's white dress or her companion's foreign gait or a hundred other details. But now you note only that the man is holding the woman's hand inside his jacket pocket. You could think her hands are cold or that they want to feel closer to each other or that it's a game, but you wonder if they aren't hiding something—a last bit of feathers or maybe just a touch of leprosy? A few remiges or a necrosis....

Why can't you see first what is right in front of you? You're a blind Tiresias. You look at the girl smiling at everyone and everything in her glassed-in office and you state, "I perceived the scene and foretold the rest: she wants to succeed, she guides her career, and is now preparing to leave for some Venice with a historian. On the train, he'll be able to paw her. She'll succeed. And she'll leave a few feathers behind. And I, Tiresias, have foresuffered." Is that all? Your arsenal allows you to see so little of the future? The sky is empty, the land a waste, and prophecies always banal.

The misfortune of having too much in one's head, I say, and, as I say it, look, you've immediately gone elsewhere, into some other time, no doubt to avoid hearing me. Well, so be it, let's talk about Griboyedov: the plaque with his name on a house shouldn't remind you of his plays so much as the fact that we turn left here. Then you go by the embassy and come to the building where friends are waiting for you.... Griboyedov has been dead for a long time.

It's not his tomb that matters, nor that the Persians killed him. From your visit to the cemetery, remember instead the warmth of the sun at dusk, the profile of a woman, her hair in a large bun, smoking and leaning on the railing, and the twinkling lights of the town below. The plaque on the house should first be an orientation point, if you don't want to get lost, and the tomb ought to remind you of life, if you want to stay alive.

If innocence is unimaginable, knowing and seeing too much are harmful, insofar as you soon won't know or see anything that you've already seen, and the contrary of which you can prove. It all consists of knowing how to impose an order on everything that settles inside you, and sometimes to succeed in forgetting it. Besides, the wild swans, like Troilus and Cressida — right? — are too precious to be used in any old way. Man of the quill, do you think you can hide behind this hodgepodge the fact that you yourself are completely flighty, incapable of inventing anything? Imagination also means seeing things as they are, in their clarity, their immediate simplicity.

You live in a world of fluttering cultural signs that you can't even control. You're sick of it, you go to pieces, and yet it might be said that you're afraid of escaping it. Would you be afraid of stinging yourself with very real nettles in order to find a human world again?

In Morocco, where I came back from, there hadn't been a war. Coming into Toulon, the first thing I had seen was scuttled ships that still hadn't been set afloat again: a funnel or a section of hull sticking up out of the water. In Rochefort, where my parents had to live, it was a little different. Surrounding the town were blockhouses. They were set underground, so that all you saw was a concrete corner, one or two loopholes, or, if you went further, a little iron door that was a powerful temptation.

But if you wanted paradise, there was the port. The dock area, where ships had been sunk, had quickly turned to mud; reeds had grown, then rushes. Six or seven years after the war, the mud had dried out, and bushes had taken root here and there. Near the docks, there were warehouses with no roofs or doors, open to the weather, and abandoned cranes and winches, boxcars where you could still see where the bullets had hit the sheet metal. Imagine it: several blocks in town deserted, with rusted machinery and these boats caught in the ground among the weeds and rushes. Words loaded with dark meanings: the Old Graving-Dock, the ramparts, the Powder Magazine, Mast Ditch, all shrines to run around and play in. Objects that used to be cartridges, rusted ammo clips in the ground or in hedges; one day, a big revolver in a ditch, totally corroded. None of these had anything to do with war. Ruins and destruction are not childhood concepts. We guessed at something menacing in the word *war* only by certain persistant signs in the adult world: He's a collaborator, they would whisper about someone or other. Or: Don't go to that store, they were collaborators. One time when I had found an insignia with a francisc on it, my mother had said: Throw away that nonsense right now. It had the feel of an accusation all the more horrible because it was beyond understanding. But what connection could it have had with the marvelous, muddy port where we played soldiers with wooden rifles?

15

At least we could have counted.

How many times had we flung our coats into the gutter so that they could step over without getting their skirts dirty? A rhetorical gesture attracted their favor, and we became their favorites. They decorated us, they armed our ships, named us Admiral-in-Chief.

We weren't any more selfish than they were, I assure you: if they gave us power, it was only for themselves. In fact, we had to return with shiploads of gold for their greater glory. Despite the nasty gossip of the Court and of History, that was our true function.

They liked us, it's true, for our adroitness, our quick wit that charmed them. We liked them too, but after each periplus it grew harder to give them the booty in exchange for mere public recognition and their private gratitude. We repressed the desire to call this game to a halt, because we grew tired of them before they disavowed us and because we knew our History: the coat trampled underfoot, the armadas destroyed, the raid on the West Indies, and, finally, the gesture of their heavily bejeweled hands giving orders to the jailor and the executioner, with the sole wages, over the centuries, of titles as bad as "rebellious admiral" or as good as "elegant adventurer" that they had the weakness or the intelligence to exploit, varying with them or with History.

Everything would have consisted of fleeing the pomp of palaces and of accepting exile and Sargassos, Saharas, the ennui, the solitude. But sooner or later it starts over: the generous gesture of the right arm throwing down the cape and the left arm twirling through the air to the ground to draw the plumed headgear over the chest: in front of them and bolt upright. And if witnesses wondered if this were arrogance or deference, they knew how to measure a cavalier's homage. One gesture signifies their approval—and soon their confidence—and it all starts over.

How many times more? How many? We were tired. We would have wanted to be a very old man, a former privateer who has finished with piracy and who has hung up his rapier. The duels and the leaping onto ships, the Court balls, the jewels on the Queen's forehead—all of it seeming insane, so far away. We would write the history of the Americas so we could dream, and all we'd need for a full life would be the warmth of a little sunlight on the hills, a cat in our lap....

Must we criticize the vanity of Essex's or Walter Raleigh's dreams, or the pointlessness of recalling them? Besides, today public gestures large and small—like headgear—have lost their flair. Missions, delegations, negotiations, treaties, mediations, procurations, trade: we no longer seek Eldorado in the Orinoco for some Gloriana, we're just errand boys for some administrative entity in a string of offices, ruled over by papers, files, and air conditioning. History has changed its face. It has the anonymous and planetary look of finances and trusts. A mentality of the procurer or usurer prevails.

At best, we're witnesses.

One day you're there, your feet in the snow and mud, for example, in Donegal Square or beneath the statue of Mickiewicz. You watch the armored cars on the square and the soldiers checking the papers of passersby. The people are scared. They know they can do nothing, and that, in our time, resistance and exile lead to nothing because they are not regulated by anything within our grasp, but by something off in offices filled with files and air conditioning spread throughout the world. There you are, collar turned up, in a little hat, feet cold, less protected from the soldiers by the statue of Mickiewicz than by a green or blue booklet in which you have a name and a number—passport, Ausweis, pasaporte, a word to know. And then violent force isn't really there, but in an intangible worldwide machine whose most powerful servants are simply cogs with no real responsibility. The patrol raids, armored cars, and curfews are simply local viscissitudes. So you lower your head or end up fired, out of work, deported, or in some obscure function. Unless, with a little luck, perhaps, you get the fleeting honor of life imprisonment or the cold bullet of a hired killer.

Maybe these days it's ridiculous to think about the great men of the past, the high-flying adventurers, especially if you yourself are of modest lineage—your father an airport night watchman with his dogs, your mother handing out books in the municipal library—grandson of poor farmers—but you should have seen my grandmother's smile as she picked flowers or laid out the first asparagus in the market—nephew of a gardener and an artisan—but when my uncle sang in his shop beneath the bridge, you could hear him all the way along the river as far as the cross on the hill: "As long as there are stars up in the sky"—waltz time—"The GrACE of your fACE was no disgrACE back then In any cASE, let's run our rACE"—rumba rhythm. . . .

Where was I? So, anyway: who can say that, in my uncle's eyes as he trimmed his grafting slips or my father's as he led his dogs, there was not the same bright and fatalistic gleam as in the eyes of the Admiral going up the Orinoco or raiding Cadiz? As the Baltic, the Black Sea, and the Pacific are just big puddles, we're all more or less of the same lineage. You too. And me. There never was an Eldorado anywhere, but tanks and soldiers were sent almost everywhere and often: ultimately no one gave the orders and nothing can be done about it. By them or you. Me either. All the philosophers in the world are not worth a forgotten refrain. We've all come down to that. But the machine never gets tired. Sometimes there are gestures of revolt against it, ephemeral jolts, but it still keeps turning. We have to know that and not think about it too much.

20

Jean and I had agreed to meet in a nearby cafe. I had been very clear about his not keeping me waiting, and he had promised not to. And now I had been waiting for an hour. I looked at the hands on my watch. The later it got, the sicker I felt. He knew it, too — I'd often told him. I knew that when he got here all he'd find to say would be "Excuse me for being late" or "You should see a doctor, really." I tried taking deep breaths to fend off the panic, a trembling deep down inside. I forced myself to read, or pretend to read. My eyes skimmed over the letters without understanding them. I tried to make myself go to the ends of the paragraphs, but I almost never got there because the slightest movement at the door made me look up.

Jean came in, elegant and smiling, and said something about car trouble and how sorry he was. We had just a minute to talk, but to him it all seemed quite simple: You're the one who should speak with the new colleague. Besides, she's coming especially to see you. It'll be easy for you to bring her around to our way of seeing things.

"I'm not so sure. We're not in a very good position. What do you know about her?"

"Not much. She's been given carte blanche, I think. A bit young for this job. She's on her way up, but you know up from down."

"Don't be silly."

"So you're down on me too?"

"Shit. You keep me waiting here for an hour, and instead of precise information, you give me this stuff."

"Listen, I told you it wasn't my fault I was late. I'm sorry it got you all worked up, but really you ought to watch it. O.K., come on, let's go."

We had all been called together for the plenary session. I know everyone, except the new girl. I count, I count again, the scene is almost set. Maurice and the Swede make solid chairmen, men of confidence, duped more than once, but solid, tense behind their awkward smiles. (Will I be like them some day, lucid and without bitterness?) Samuel is too nice, too romantic to get very far. The two from Brussels came on the same train and with—to protect themselves—the same mocking look. Then there is Maria, her demeanor serious but full of grace. Miss Buttons my old friend, whose laugh is as big as her hats. Two others, not very important supernumeraries. Matt's missing. He's capable of letting you down, he who yesterday said that there's no point in taking cover because sooner or later you have to settle your accounts with others, with yourself.

We're ready for a ritual that hardly ever changes. We'll always agree, generally at the expense of one among us. Since we know what is possible and what isn't, we almost always win, no? We're wary of new groundrules and newcomers. As for me, who passes for one of the most capable, I'm careful not to lose when I know I can't win.

Shortly after Matt, the new colleague arrives in a red and blue dress with impatiens appliqued, relaxed and wearing a smile, younger, maybe a lot younger than me. So she's the one with whom I'm going to have to discuss, argue, and beat around the bush. The attendance sheet is signed, we have our chits, we can start the meeting.

Right away, the new girl opens. My cards aren't strong, so I just call. Jean raises, but almost always to counter me and to keep me from raising her, as if there's a secret understanding between them. The others fold or discard as if they're all ganging up on me. One of them sandbags and another is poker-faced. There doesn't seem to be any way for me to win these hands. Who'll help me? Matt, the true blind prophet, doesn't even seem to see I'm caught in the middle. The shrewder Miss Buttons catches on, but waits too long to do anything about it. Her neighbor offers only a look that means "Break the bank, stud! And forget your penny ante." What game are we playing here? Isn't it a misdeal? I'm tired. The game seems pointless. I know how to shuffle the cards and get back in the game, but I no longer have the memory I used to have. The deal passes, luck turns. It's not my deal now, my hot hand gone, high hand gone. One of these days I'll be screwed.

During the coffee break, I suddenly remember the following: from fourteen to seventeen, I corresponded with a girl my own age. We diligently talked about the good and bad weather and sometimes we exchanged little gifts (I remember a handkerchief with my initials embroidered on it for my birthday). When I was sent to Oxford, she suggested that we finally meet, and I accepted her invitation to visit her parents on a Sunday. So as not to wait alone in a large station like Paddington, she had asked her brother to go with her. They waited all morning—as late as noon, she later wrote me. I had to offer some excuse for not having come, but after that I never did go to meet her. Our correspondence ended not long after and I quickly forgot even her name. Why had that old incident suddenly come back to me? After all those years, I thought about the little Londoner again, certainly in her prettiest dress, seeing the Oxford trains come in one after another, and her impatience, her disappointment.... Shame rises in me, absurdly. It would have nauseated me if the immediate situation hadn't called me back.

Partners, adversaries, all the colleagues sit down again

around the table. Jean didn't even come over to say a word to me. I saw him chatting with the new girl. What does he want from her? I'm tired. Nervousness makes me quiver slightly. I've always drawn my self-assurance from the confidence others show in me, and now I think they're making fun of me. Finally they must have understood that I was faking it. The red and blue dress returned. We started again. What should I do? Fling myself at her knees, throw my arms around her legs, and bury my face in the folds of her dress as I beg her: "O Pallas, forgive me. I am your knave." What a hullaballoo that'd make! And she would scornfully brush me aside: "Poor little bluffer, do you think you're Ogier the Dane? We have no need for gallant knights. There are no more queens or cavaliers-in-waiting. If there are still knaves, they're always menials, lackeys." The queen would not turn her pure profile toward me, would not toss me her red flower with its three lanceolated leaves. Why would I do that? Why? After all, to my left there is nothing but the obstinate face of a functionary pleased with her dress and concerned with her career. Me, I hardly ever cared about mine. Oh well, when I'm gone, maybe my opponents will remember me. To flee, to escape is impossible. All that I can do is wait it out and maintain my bluff for the last hand, an hour or two at most.

With a hat for the sun and some boots for the rattlesnakes, you can plunge in among the rocky thickets. Broken columns, steps, sections of dim frieze can suddenly emerge in a clearing. The only things that live in the ruins at Dzibilchaltun are insects and various reptiles, especially iguanas and those big snakes the Indian called *boas* a few minutes ago. Or, growing way up on the big crumbling pile of quarry stone, bushes and cacti. Still, there are temples beneath the piles, temples men built seventeen centuries ago.

Brushing's not enough and the comb would pull too hard. In plunging my fingers into your hair to untangle it, I rediscover the sliding of the fresh-water plants of my adolescence: you'd part them with your hands as you swam and you'd feel them brushing along your whole body. But now I'm far from a page boy. I'm like a mule hitched to a millstone, going around in a circle for the benefit of philistines. The blinders make my eyes deader than the eyes of the blind, since I can't imagine anything: all I can see is you, you.

You love your supple hair, which has to be cut regularly to retain its beauty. In our time, women keep their hair for themselves; a Berenice doesn't offer it to Venus anymore, even for Callimachus or Catullus. But men have to have theirs cut; it's supposed to be for their own good. An old David ends up pursuing an adventurous Absalom who always dies with his beautiful hair caught in the branches of an oak tree.... And yet, now that I'm standing here holding a pair of scissors, don't you consider, with my fingertips gently stroking your neck, don't you consider the possibility that three or four bites of these scissors could, in retaliation, quickly ravage your hair and take away the power of its charm? It doesn't matter—it's too late to shake the columns of the temple.

I work carefully, making the curls even. I go from lock to lock, leaving not a single split end. Then I brush it until it shines. My role is modest and transitory, but it gives me the privilege of seeing the down on your nape. I'm neither your valet nor your service man. I can't offer you white pages with polished and elegant words, only the cajoling chitchat of hairdressers.

28

Packed in its cottony husk, a horse chestnut. Under the sheets, under the covers, it's pleasantly warm, and the true source of warmth is that other body, beside you. Above the roundness of shoulder and the wavy hair spread across the pillow, you see the window's rectangle where day is beginning to rise. Outside, the wind makes the trees rustle, and you hear the rain, too. It's nice, it's warm. But beyond the shoulder, the glimmering at the window has an airport blinking in the early morning. In the airports, it's still night or already night. You arrive or leave again alone. The raw, impersonal light, the searchlights, the brightly lit ramps, the colored runway lights can't part the ambient darkness, the good, the true night. A memory comes back: an inscription on the lintel of a manor house window in Loir-et-Cher: *Before leaving.*

Day is about to break. It's a bit cold in the room, but a lot warmer in the bed, dovetailed into each other. My legs follow the angle of hers: the backs of her thighs, the bent knees, the calves. The lower part of the belly is packed, with an animal pleasure, against the roundness of her behind, and the chest against her back. The temperature of the two bodies is the same and the contact is so close that neither can tell where the bodies end. One of the arms lies across her body, the elbow pressing against her hip and the forearm on her belly that rises slightly in the rhythm of breathing. Her two hands hold the wrist pressed against her chest, the hand closed over one breast, as if holding a beating heart.

You start to see, as daylight begins to filter through the window. It'll be day soon. For the moment, the eyes make out, a few inches away, only the whiteness of the sheets and a dim mass of hair. You can plunge your face into the warm scent of the hair to look for a little leftover night, or press your lips to the base of the nape to feel her hips move and her hands squeeze the arm tighter against her breast.

Day breaks. You hear cars. You'd like to ignore it, to stay like an animal. Any moment the alarm will go off, and already a hint of distress is working its way between the bodies. You have to get up, go, and pick up living like a man again.

30

The point is not, you say, to take a nice trip so you can write a book: I have to draw up a detailed and itemized report of my mission. When I turn in this report, they'll see about paying me, this fact being quite secondary when they're dealing with a writer. I'll have to justify my comings and goings to the accounting office, which will determine the amount, because there's no way they'll simply pay me a flat fee. Since I don't keep a diary, I've done so many things that I no longer know which I've actually done and which I've dreamed. For one long month on the road I have only a few sentences scribbled in a notebook, some ideas and impressions I promised myself I'd continue or develop later, but now, like the dream you forget by the end of the day, I no longer know what they refer to or for whom they were intended. Lost among names and telephone numbers that have lost their meaning. By contract. All that remain of my contracts are quick impressions and notations that have become enigmatic:

I won't be the good Samaritan who'll help you get rid of yourself, that is to say your father, your mother, your sisters, and a few other people you envy, scorn, or despise. Hell is the Dallas airport at a perpetual three A.M. Hardness of the dancer's thighs in their impersonal roundness. I'm such a stranger to myself that even my own smell disgusts me when I go to the crapper. Two big paintings and a smaller one with colors very.... Do I stand there stock still, if time has no space, or am I a cycle? Or else a line? In fact, my time, my life is a cycloid. SECOND DRAFT. I will watch you in the gait of a passerby, the figure of an assistant in a store, the profile of a stranger sitting next to me in the subway; you can go now; you will never be gone. There is a draft: I will close the door when I leave. In the train an old lady says to her husband, "Tous les noisetiers ont des chatons." All the hazel trees have kittens? Die Hazelnuszsträucher haben Kätzschen? Avellanos con gatitos?

Furthermore, on a stale-dated check stamped Nov. 16 '76, the word THANATOS in capital letters. Also:

As her mouth is contorted on the harmonica and the sun on her bandana.

That's all the marvelous anthology pages I've brought back from a nice trip. If by chance a sentence is good, it's probably because it was copied from something I read. And here I am at the end of a pointless odyssey, head empty, pockets empty, but with contracts fulfilled for you. And I'm not the first one, either: "To speak French with you, you must open your hand. Thus my wallet becomes for me the sole organ through which I can clarify the difficulties of the Bible, and make the Centuries of Nostradamus as easy for you as the Pater. Finally, miss, it is of you alone that verily it may be said 'Nothing for nothing.'" At actual cost. I traveled at actual cost and now I must assemble tickets, receipts, notes, bills: for 1,311 miles, gas vouchers from Gulf and Texaco, Huybensz and Lipucci, and fifty toll receipts, two Surtram tickets, stubs from parking lots in New Haven, Washington, Philadelphia, and San Antonio. But I can't find the rental contract for the Oldsmobile, so I won't be reimbursed for that. Two L.I. Railroad tickets: I'll have to explain that I have only the outbound tickets because the conductor collects the tickets on the way back into New York. Two Greyhound tickets. And airline tickets, reimbursable or not: American Airlines, two Delta, Texas International, two Braniff, Eastern, two TWA, three Cruzeiro, two Varig, Avianca, two Air France. And then receipts, bits of nondescript paper stamped Caracas, Sulphur Springs, Berkeley, Stedelijk Museum, Annandale-on-Hudson, M.A.S.P.: Di Cavalcanti. I have carefully collected whatever I have been able to learn of the story, as Goethe says. (Ah, Charlotte, Charlotte!

Where are you? Help me. Charlotte, I haven't forgotten the blondness of your hair. Idiot: Charlotte is an airport where the gawky silhouette of your friend Padgett is waiting, it's a city in North Carolina. Carolyn! Carolyn! I haven't forgotten the blondness of your hair. Completely insane, this guy.) I say no more. Don't let yourself be mad at me. "The only courtesy I ask of you is that you tear me so gently that I can pretend not to feel it."

34

Sure, words are just words, sounds uttered in the void, little ants frozen against the whiteness, but that's not all. We shouldn't ask too much of them or despise them: the power of words doesn't allow us to start life over, they don't create anything, they don't preserve anything, but they allow something to pass among people. We shouldn't be too stingy with them: when you're old your voice will be thick with all the words you didn't say, just as your fingers will be swollen with all the gestures you didn't make.

Perhaps it isn't exactly what words say that matters, but that they're said to someone. The proof of this is that all subjects are good.

I remember what someone once told me on a bus. Sitting next to me was a plain, unpretentious woman of no particular age. She had been visiting her parents in Brownsville. Because of my somewhat drawling accent, she thought I was a compatriot. Her husband ran a garage in the North, but he was going to retire soon. Her children were grown, and she was thinking about moving back home. Why did she tell me that? No doubt it was easier for her to talk to a stranger. She had been engaged to a boy who was sent to Korea. He was there for two years. When he came back, she had moved up North, married to someone else. A few years later, he suddenly knocked at her door. She was scared, but she opened the door anyway. Nothing happened. He said he just wanted to know how she was getting along. And the two men agreed that things like this happen sometimes. That was it. She shook hands with me when I got off at Saint Louis. Not very exciting, is it? But that's not the point. That was several years ago, but I haven't forgotten.

All words are good. Often they stay in our memories longer than the faces of the people who said them. If the life of cats in a cemetery doesn't sound to you like a good subject, you're wrong, because there's a man, far away from here, a Guarani fisherman who remembers me only because of it. Naturally, I don't speak Guarani, but because he and I knew a little Spanish, we were more or less able to talk. He offered me some of his maté and I felt quite honored. I don't recall how it came up, but in any case I was explaining to him that in Paris, at Père Lachaise, there are old women who feed the hundreds of cats that live there, half wild. It may seem ridiculous to be in Paraná and talking about the cats in Parisian cemeteries, but that was precisely what really interested my friend of one hour. He wanted to know where these cats came from, what the women gave them to eat, if all the cemeteries in Europe were like that. He asked a lot of other questions I did my best to answer. (You see, it's not hard: when you meet a Guarani fisherman, just talk to him about cemetery cats....)

Let's not joke around too much with words.

To experience an event, to tell someone about it, and to write about it are three unrelated acts. The first is the only authentic one. The second can lie with flowery words, but, as I said, it's very important for others and oneself. As for the last one, which results in darkened leaves, I'm less sure of its importance, although dead leaves are sometimes nice to look at. They can also be put in books or used to make a fire. So they're not completely useless, right?

37

It's the usual spectacle you see in the slums of big cities. Paper trash, beer cans, children dragging along in the dust. A few old people watch them from the doorway shade. Beale Street is a big street lined with mangy stores that are just pawnshops, advertising

DIAMONDS REVOLVERS GUITARRS

SEWING MACHINES

ETC.

In fact, there's everything in the window. The diamonds are of course fake, but the rest are quite real. You can find umbrellas and operating tables. But the only beautiful chance encounter happens up the street, in a little square that is both spic-and-span and preposterous: two trees, two benches, and between them a man in new clothes and shoes, a trumpet in his hand:

WILLIAM CHRISTOPHER HANDY

1873–1958

COMPOSER

38 COMPLETE FICTION SERGE FAUCHEREAU

Around the square, nothing but empty lots and rubbish, a lot of beams and rotten boards, plaster and garbage. The man with the trumpet is on a pedestal of black stone. He's been all duded up with a smile and a double-breasted jacket so he could be poured in bronze in the middle of a dump. He has to wait until the Beale Street pawnshops and stinking bars cave in, until the upper crust and nice neighborhoods with banks get this far. He's been given nice clothes in advance. Handy. That's convenient. Until then, how many times will it be necessary to kill Martin Luther King?

In this cove surrounded by oblique walls, setting up a port had been easy. All they had to do was build two staggered jetties to break the strong waves. Now the basin holds only a few old boats of no great use and some reeds. The pier is overgrown with weeds. Right behind the cliff are the ruins of big stone buildings whose color blends into the surrounding rocks and bushes. The missing roofs let you see the arrangement of walls and partitions. Above this first level, other tiers rise above the cliffs, more exposed to the weather; they blend pillars and stretches of wall with freakish outlines. Still further off, isolated buildings yawn to the open sky. There are no windows. The big doors are dark holes that sometimes spit out bushes.

No one. Heavy with mud and kelp, the very water is dead. All you hear is the cry of seagulls. High in the sky, buzzards wheel, their wings unmoving. It could have been like this forever, quiet and beautiful, as at Luxor or Angkor Wat.

Yesterday an old man explained to me that it had been a

big stone-crushing factory. There used to be a dump-car train that came right up here to get the gravel. You could still find some of the rails in the grass. He himself had worked here before the war. But the war had nothing to do with it: one day, they stopped filling the warehouses and they stopped the crushers. He doesn't know why. The workers left. The village was abandoned. And he too left Porthgain to work in Cardiff. Storms and salt air did the rest in a few dozen years. Centuries from now it will look exactly the same.

In six or seven years I saw her in only two summer dresses, a white one with blue stripes and a pink one with little checks (these made her the prettiest, no?). On her feet I never saw anything but sandals and low-cut shoes called "ballerinas." I think the "sand clog" style lasted less than two years: they were little shoes in white perforated leather with wooden soles. She wanted some. She looked at them in shop windows. Her desire became so strong that she admitted it to me. But her parents weren't any richer than mine, and the purchase of a pair of sand clogs seemed less important to them than it did to their daughter. She never got them. After that the style changed. Then she was seventeen, then eighteen, then nineteen, then twenty, and adult life led us our own ways and I never saw her again. But I remember how much she wanted a pair of sand clogs.

So? What's the point of overdramatizing, of digging up the past? Memories are only vestiges, of no interest to the present. Since the bottom of memory is moving sand, let the memories disappear. Or do you think it's possible today to take a pair of outdated shoes to someone whom, after a quarter of a century, you wouldn't even recognize? Dig too deep and all you get is a foretaste of the earth you'll have between your teeth. When all that remains of you is a few pieces of bone that a farmer in the distant future turns over with his spade, he'll be wise enough to leave them in the ground — and you'll pass into the plants and into peace.

There's no doubt that a distant memory is useless. It's a fragment that has lost its life and almost all its meaning, like this little piece of pottery I brought back from an archeological site in Tomis a few years ago, and which is over there, lying on the corner of the desk. I just keep it, without attaching too much importance to it. Anyway, everything we dig up from the earth will go back into it.

43

Hell is the section where they keep the forbidden books locked up, but Hell isn't reserved for only a few books. Beneath nine cupolas, a little light slips in through three stained-glass windows. For decoration, medallions of various Dantes and Shakespeares set in plaster of Paris, and six large fresco panels with not very believable trees: did they want the visitor to think he was outside the crypt? And then, books by the thousands, by the millions, books made of pulped plants and covered with the skins of dead animals. A big cemetery jealously guarded by conservators: they conserve, in fact they embalm—hence the smell of dust and old leather. These "civil" servants stand guard: the books, manuscripts, and prints can be seen only by initiates who are deemed worthy of it. Ideally they wouldn't show anything to anyone, so the more rare and precious a thing is, the less they want to bring it out into the light. They themselves are there to oversee things, not see them.

The readers are in a studious torpor. With an emergency scholarship or to forget what year it is, these prospectors abandon themselves to burrowing, the mother of every coroner's curiosity. Day by day, the most cunning of them foment their careers and scavenge the works of others. Most of them, gnawing their nails, nibble with trembling lips at what they read. A philosophical few drowse. In X years, when I'll be long dead, perhaps one of them will consult one of my books for a footnote.... But I would have really loved to have been leafed through at a bookseller's outdoor stand, along the Seine, among people strolling along, under trees that are really alive!

45

The red two-door Ford is in this parking lot for the last time. Its occupant has rolled down the window and is looking at the man who is leaning against the door, pushing against it with his left hand. She has put her hand on his, and this last gesture is like the first. In fact, everything begins banally, a chance meeting, thanks, let's say, to a mutual friend. He looks so lonely and helpless that during his second visit she touches his hand tenderly. He takes that hand and holds it for a while, then she presses against him, and so forth: with a few variations, all stories repeat each other. They know it's a liaison doomed to failure, but that doesn't matter. Everything happens in a few days and is resolved in a departure in which both of them feel, deep down, only a slight trembling. That's the way it is, in life and in novels. So the young woman is turned toward him, her brown hair touches the collar of her summer dress, and she is smiling sadly, still with a winsome glint, perhaps to keep from crying. He, the stranger passing through, is looking at her seriously, as if to keep her features from fading from his memory. For several months he'll send her postcards from some Paris or Copenhagen, then all that'll remain will be this snapshot set in memory, a virtual image.

The sky is an intense blue and the sun cuts hard shadows on the car, on the face of the young woman at the wheel, and on that of the man in blue who is leaning toward her at the door, his eyes fastened on her but already laced with lines: Air France, KLM, Braniff, Amtrak, whatever, a tragic and absurd man whose place is elsewhere. (So what was his name? Incomprehensible, overbearing, and timid, always flanked by some blond or else that brunette who looked you over from up there and bragged in public about her prowess with him, and her husband who smiled, how did I look, we had no future together, and the time those two girls had argued just a few feet away from my place, fortunately there was Luis Enrique later, I think.) The moment of separation has remained suspended like a clear snapshot: two people in a parking lot and one of them leaning toward the one sitting in a red Ford. There are also two other people frozen in the background: they're friends who came along with him or who are leaving with him or, rather, it's him again, recognizable by his blue clothes, with a woman.

The setting is that of a new town with perpendicular and empty streets and avenues, with houses, trees, streetlights, and telephone poles stretching out into the infinite suburbs. A parking lot at the corner of a 23rd or 25th Street, beneath a raw light. The man leaning against the car door is looking inside at the young woman in a pink dress who has put her hand on his. He sees her mournful smile in a pleasantly round face framed with wavy, tawny blond hair. (Complicated and sentimental little person who cries easily, crying from tenderness or crying from rage at her frigidity, her name is Susan; no, Maria; or else Carole; it hardly matters. I let her go back to the baroque music albums inherited from her ex-husband, whose name was Douglas, Otto, or Carlos, or else from her friend Peter, or her old friend Jean-Pierre; I'll never be one of them.) He knows that in no time he'll be nothing to her and that he's leaving the way cheap novels end, taking with him only the roundness of a thigh, the slightly self-conscious softness of a voice, and a goodbye through the rolled-down window of a red Ford on a sunny day.

That's all ordinary, and it's fine that way. We're in the place common to us all. What we think of as original is simply a cliché that hasn't gotten around. The objects and situations don't matter. It's enough to take one of those squares in any of the old capitals: there's a monument in the middle, with shops, restaurants, and cafes all around, and still, even at night, a constant flow of people and vehicles; then, at a busy outdoor cafe, two people again, man and woman: her eyes follow the neon lights and sidewalk commotion, looking thoughtful with a slightly bitter smile, while he rocks in his chair and looks at his glass, or else at the watch and metal band around the young woman's wrist, both of them easing their solitude against that of the other. It is vital to leave the scene to itself, the antithesis of the red Ford with the frozen couples, but still a photoroman cliché. And it's fine that way. You have a terrific desire to escape the daily bathos, you have such a distrust of the conventional, of the usual order of things and people that you don't really live anymore. But the art of living, like art itself, consists precisely in the knowledge and understanding of clichés, as you've been told: *stupid paintings, pictures of clowns, outdated literature, inane books.*

"Gare Saint-Lazare" is the title, the size about three by four feet. A young woman in blue with long tawny hair pulled back to reveal the face and the slightly large ears with earrings that cast a shadow on her cheek. She's holding an open book while she waits, sitting near the iron fence. Also on her knees is a folded fan and a puppy, a little cocker or spaniel with its eyes closed. Who is she? The Anglo-Saxon governess of the little girl next to her? The big sister? The little girl, turning her back to us, has put her bunch of grapes on the stone and now looks across at the trains and the smoke, gripping the black bars at the risk of getting her pretty dress dirty. The young woman in blue has glanced up from her book and is looking toward me. She's smiling slightly. She doesn't understand that I've chosen to stop in front of her. 1873. Manet. Just as the light from a dead star reaches us today in all its intensity, there's the space of a century in the look we exchange. The more I stare at her, the more I study her dark eyes, the more I sense a light pink rising in her cheeks. I'm going to get up from the bench where I'm writing this on the back of a handbill. Leave so I won't embarrass her.

Train stations and airports always make me edgy. Still, I'm a traveler with no particular habits: on the train I sit anywhere, with maybe a slight preference for the aisle seat so I can get up and move around; and on the plane I don't mind the seat over the wing, even if the landscape gets cut diagonally by the aluminum. But I never hear a train in the distance without being moved (the cry of Russian trains is the only one that's as beautiful as that of American trains), and it's the plane I don't take that I pay close attention to as it rolls down the runway, along the ground-lights, rises easily, retracts its wheels into its belly, and plunges into a spongy sky....

Rather than the one I should take, I'd naturally prefer any other train or plane going anywhere, especially if I know that among the people who'll be waiting where I'm going, no one will be there for me. No one was waiting for me in Rio—a hostess helped me—and I don't like Rome, where I had to go only once, because, having arrived alone, I quickly snuck out, alone.

Vast or improvised but interchangeable around the world, train stations and airports are not just places for arrival and departure. They have people who are neither arriving nor departing: they're waiting. And some of them will have come for nothing. They're waiting and you pay attention to them only if you're sure that among them you'll find the face of a friend, a relative, a colleague, or, for lack of someone better, an official representative sent to pick you up. One place is as good as the next. What matters is that someone's waiting for you.

52

There are only a few gestures we can make. You have to make them, like everyone else, or you will not communicate and you will live only for yourself. Who do you think you are, not to accept this?

There rises in him a groundswell as he looks at her and wants to tell her he understands her sorrow and her problems, how he feels close to her and that he feels the same confusion and, and, he thinks only of the usual words and gestures, which his timidity, his pride, his cowardice resist. The bus drove through the cold of Kalinin Avenue; at the stops, some people got on, others got off; everything calm and normal. She looks straight ahead, face set. What should he do? Maybe take her hand. But he doesn't want to, he doesn't know how to, he. Finally, just a light undertow: he taps his fingertips on her forearm. She turns her closed face toward him: "What is it?" Even the sea spray is probably just that bit of melted snow on the windowpane. "Nothing," he says.

After one of those nights when you dream that you're still a child, I wake up a bit stiff, neck aching, head foggy. For a moment I just lie there, postponing the start of the day. I think about last night's nightmares and of my not very satisfying life moving from one place to another. But I'm happy anyway with the little sunlight coming through the windows overlooking Ninth Avenue.

And then Bill comes in the room, lounging in his pajamas and singing an old musical comedy number: Good morning, good mo-o-orning, good morning to you! Good, the day augers well, I can get up cheerfully.

Coffee and rolls suddenly bring me back to life. Also, I look through the morning paper for this Saturday, the seventh of March. There is news meant for me. Why must there be, amidst wars, crimes, and the usual cataclysms, something waiting for me — me? But there they are, side by side: "Maria Jolas, 94, translator and founder of magazine in Paris" and "Eddie Durham, trombonist, member of Count Basie orchestra."

I had met Maria Jolas a dozen or so years ago, but suddenly it seemed like yesterday. She had invited me to her apartment on the Rue de Rennes. I can see myself on the landing, waiting at her door. It was opened by a big heavy woman. She explained how, with her husband, she did *transition* magazine. She showed me documents and drawings. She spoke of Schwitters, Arp, or Joyce as if she had just seen them, and referred to Soupault, who was four or five years younger than her, as "that boy." And so she described the people of the twenties and thirties and the canteen called La Marseilleise she opened in New York for French refugees during the war. She recalled all these events without regret, often with amusement. Her enthusiasm was even more contagious when she talked about her projects, her next trip, some novel she's translating into English, or some other one she's tempted to translate.

Eddie Durham is another matter, further back in time, in my greener days. I was seventeen. I scrimped and saved so I could buy jazz records. The first were the ones I loved most: Kid Ory, Bechet, Beiderbecke, Armstrong of course, and even an Englishman, Lyttleton. There were long discussions with my friend Jean-Claude: which record to buy —since we had money for just one—Muggsy Spanier or Count Basie? We brought the precious acquisition back home and listened to it while carefully studying the musicians' names on the jacket. That's how I'd known about

Eddie Durham's trombone since way back. At eighty, he was getting ready to appear in concert. Now he's dead, like Maria Jolas.

I wasn't very close to them, obviously, but with their disappearances a little of my life crumbles, yesterday becomes past tense. Deaths bring us closer to our own death, but above all we must keep in mind that certain people remained at the heart of life right up to the last instant: they were translating, they were building, they were making music, for others. Let's go, you, still alive, straighten up, do something, or at least go out to take advantage of this bit of sunlight in the street.

FROM

DISPLACEMENTS

TRANSLATED BY JOHN ASHBERY

First I see myself having just emerged from the warmth of the underground corridors of the Metro, climbing a street I don't know, leading I don't know where. A very long street where I walk straight ahead, passing dozens of doors, each with its number.

Then I was standing in front of a school building, waiting on the sidewalk across the street, watching, sorting out the silhouettes of children from those of men and women. I couldn't say whether I was worried, nervous. I think that above all I was cold. In dreams we never ask ourselves questions. I was waiting, that's all.

Then, suddenly someone was coming toward me. Yes, it was the one I had been waiting for, across the street. We were seventeen or a hundred and seven years old. The two-way traffic prevented us from crossing. I could make out only a smile, but not the features of the face, concealed behind thick dark glasses. Finally it was I who was able to cross between the cars. Was it me? Awkward handshake, it seemed. I didn't hear the first words we exchanged.

They walked down the long street, side by side, without

looking at each other, as though a glance would have petrified them, with a space of air cold as a sword between them. Looking for a place to sit down, grab a bite.

A restaurant. As it wasn't yet dinner time, the large room was empty and offered only rows of tables covered with white cloths, separated by aisles. A space seemed to be reserved: A table like the others was offered them; their names weren't on it but there were little bouquets of forget-me-nots and some kind of narcissus.

At that point no one knows where one is. A landmark is needed, some kind of light. But isn't it always after the fact that events and dreams are lit up? At the moment one saw only the truth, without the aid of a lighthouse. Well, then ... But I would like to add that truth itself, like love, is blind; or is it justice? A lighthouse would be of no use to her. She is nude because she is young and emerging from a well, or else because she is an old philosopher who has renounced appearances. Yes, that's it. But I would also like to add that the truth is as naked as Venus emerging from the waves— or might one prefer that she be wearing, according to the modesty and styles of the period, a two-piece red-and-white bathing suit? (Why red and white? Perhaps because they are the colors of fire and water, passion and fulfillment, revolution and reaction, the donkey and the goose, wine and bread; I don't know).

It could be two people who had known, loved each other centuries or decades earlier, some Paolo and Francesca:

(There is no sharper pain than that of memory. We were reading one day a story of Lancelot. We were alone and very young. And then later on: That day we read no more.) Then age and time mingled in it, and society which imposes its order on children's games. One could scarcely believe that, in truth, those who were meeting there were the descendants of those adolescents long ago. The truth? Be aware that she is holding up a mirror and, since she lacks love's absent-mindedness, this always clean though fogged mirror is turned toward you. Thus it is I whom I saw at that table in the restaurant.

I observed myself closely and clearly realized the quandary I was in: that of the solitary customer who stares at his beer so as not to see his image reflected in the mirrors of the bar. He didn't know where to aim his gaze convincingly so as to avoid the face and the gaze opposite him. Better to lower one's eyes toward the starched tablecloth where the ritual had placed the dishes for the meal, and the flowers for the eye and for symbolism. Then comes the moment to attack the food for the body and the soul. Crudités and mixed vegetables, Madame; sweetbreads and cream sauce, Monsieur. Vittles, grub, blowout. Meeting again. Nuptials, churching, brats. Funerals. Time passes quickly from the thymus to tired features, from bare feet in the grass to carpet slippers on the waxed floor. Venus in furs will put her mothballed heart in slipcovers like an arm chair. For lack of the greenness of the Age of Gold we have the greenery of vinegared salads. As for the other bloke who seems to have been bumped off by the Bacchantes—no more juice in the electric guitar, old buddy—let him eat his sweetbreads then.

So they ate, all the while inquiring about each other and a more or less peaceful, more or less agitated life, and memories mingled with polite questions. Moderation, correctness. Enough of tragedies, comedies, farces, glittering trifles, idylls; to hell with make-up and accessories, the torch of liberty and the mirror of truth. In the shadow theater God knows that a minimum is sufficient.

I was there: I saw everything. To make a long story short there are only two persons who met again after a long time and looked at each other across the tablecloth, the food and the flowers, and there was nothing extraordinary in this: still-familiar faces whose complexion is rendered paler and more uniform by the neon, the eyes a little sunken perhaps, where I wanted to believe that the spark had stayed the same. What vanity!

PARIS, 4 MARCH 93

POST-SCRIPTUM: Dante's *Inferno* seems to have given its shape more or less to this funereal ceremony, but perhaps it is also the *Vita Nuova*.

Incipit Vita Nova.

The economic war spares nobody. On all the continents, the conquerors' handwriting spurts up along the highways and in the cities, tall signboards blazing day and night: Coca Cola, American Express, Benetton, Fuji, Lancôme, MacDonald's. The newspaper *Moscow* is for sale entirely in English. Television proclaims in color with supportive smiles the grandeur of Omo, Head & Shoulders and other detergents and deodorants. Money has no smell and imposes an ideal.

The words that print themselves on television screens, in display windows and advertisements in the unknown lettering of the people who live here have a force and a meaning which don't come through when they are deciphered. These are penciled arabesques respected both by the peasant woman who has come to the city to sell a few kilos of potatoes and by the hotel porter who knows a few scraps of western languages. It's sufficient that they are legible to local and foreign businessmen, to gilded youth and to the various underworld professionals.

And I who walk back up Tverskaia Street (formerly Gorky Avenue, too bad about him), I'm probably wrong to ask myself pragmatic questions. What I want to know about public writing is of no interest to the life that's here. I have nothing to sell, I buy nothing, and what I write is meant neither for businessmen nor the nouveaux riches nor for the petty crooks. As for the porter and the peasant with her potatoes, they have other, more urgent preoccupations. Whosoever writes, isn't he on the side of those who inscribe their trademark, a slogan or graffiti?

At the end of the avenue where the industrial fumes and neon signs have chased away the horses of the sun, the Marlboro cowboy lights up a cigarette while holding the reins of something one doesn't see. One expects the sky to retire, like a manuscript that is being rolled up.

MOSCOW, 29 MARCH 1993

When you are very old and your hair is entirely white, rambling on gently about your memories, perhaps my name will come to your lips. And if someone asks who it was, you'll answer: "He was a French writer, we did a lot of things together, a French writer." We become discreet, as we get older, about the carousing, the debauchery, the drinking bouts. As for me, I'll be underground, a phantom without bones. So, if I happen to run into Ronsard in the myrtle-infested shadows, he won't begrudge my having plagiarized a sonnet (after all, he pardoned Yeats who was a greater thief than I). Therefore, regret nothing: the roses of life, we gathered a lot of them even so.

—AFTER A SECOND FRENCH WRITER
ISLINGTON, 1989

66

Death is gentler in the Far East because the dead continue to look after the affairs of the living. If something goes awry, it's customary to attribute it to the intervention of dissatisfied ancestors. Then it becomes necessary to change the location of the tomb or else make some special offering, according to the counsels of the shaman who summons spirits and interrogates them during the course of a complex and kindly ritual.

In the hospital room where my father spent his final hours, the doctors, with my consent, prevented him from suffering and, above all, from thinking. It was a matter of letting him depart without pain and without distress. The mechanism that regularly injected him with morphine accomplished its task, objectively. They unplugged it when the heart whose suffering it relieved stopped beating. No doubt it has served many times since then. In the Occident, machines endure longer than spirits. In any case, my father, who didn't like getting mixed up in other people's affairs, wanted to be cremated and his ashes scattered so there would be nothing left to bother those who survived him.

One has to choose this or that, here or there, in one sense or another. Foolish people like me would like to have the comfort of technology along with the friendship of the timeless. For the people of the Far East, life and death coexist, cooperate. For me, the Occidental, there are distinct and antithetical facts which can't accommodate each other.

There have been many times when I would have liked to know my father's opinion. But since, no more than I, he didn't believe in spirits, neither tomb nor urn mark his last resting place. There remains only his watch, which he gave me a few days before going into the hospital; he felt more tired than ill, and, as time weighed heavy on him, he wanted to be rid of it.

I'm constantly looking at time—when I'm waiting for someone, for a train or a plane—and it's not often that I think of my father. The watch is a utilitarian mechanism whose symbolism has been punctiliously forgotten. Materialist time blots out relics and chases ghosts away.

SEOUL, 11 MAY 1993

68

Children, we were children, Heine says, and nothing was serious but our games. Now we walk calmly, talking about mortgages, exchanging opinions on the buying of a piece of clothing for our respective mates. The problem with having, you know ... and, as Heine says, the price of coffee has gone up again.

We walk on, each looking straight ahead. But *I* know. I haven't forgotten. To the eyes and fingers of my memory a still-familiar silhouette has emerged, standing before a mirror, arms raised to put her hair up, her supple and eager body outlined by peach-colored undies and a scanty matching camisole. I won't say anything. Besides, we were children, children whose sleep wasn't bothered by coffee, nor money, nor clothes, nor fickleness. I'm not saying anything about it. Nothing to do with houses or mortgages. Everything flies away, time, love, and faithfulness, as Heine says, and the price of coffee.

TOKYO, 11 JULY 1993

69

The first images of my life are of departure. I had quickly been taken away from my natal city and the risk of bombardments to flee toward a port in the south; and then a long crossing in an old tub till we reached Algeria and then Morocco. I was so little that I have no memory of it, but the taste for movement must have already entered me.

The earliest memory I can recall is this: when my father left, we saw the column of Algerian cavalry moving away along the trail for a long time. They were singing. At the moment when they began to disappear over the top of the erg, someone guessed they were signaling to us; so we too waved goodbye to them. We heard them singing for a while, far away, and then it was another hour before the dust settled behind them.

One never leaves a place without a little anxiety. Last evening in Paris, the day before in London, today in Florence, one ought to be used to it, but no. I'd wave if there was anyone to notice me.

FIESOLE, 13 DECEMBER 1993

A television program about the peak of Teyde that I visited two months ago. I watch it with as much attention as when I was actually there. I see better because the TV camera sweeps across panoramas and zeroes in on details of the mountain that I hadn't noticed when I was walking there. I have the impression that I am learning more than when I passed through those same places. But, despite the movement and the color, these images that are unfurling now are dead; slouched against a pillow, passive, I don't live off them.

I knew someone who had written a book which quickly became a classic on American poetry of his time, without ever having met the poets he discussed, or even setting foot in America. So? Like the documentary on the peak of Teyde, the book was certainly rich in information, but, inevitably, the essential was missing: life, the very poetry that neither quotations nor reproductions nor explications can replace. Outside of the poem, poetry is as difficult to communicate as the dry and acrid heat of the volcanic rock under the soil or the squirting of latex from the bristling euphorbia, fragile and bleeding white when you brush against them in passing.

VILLEJUIF, MARCH 1994

72

All the cities, all the places you never go back to, nothing but a name remains of them or sometimes a detail, a tiny inconsequential fact. The tall chestnut trees one saw from the window at Surgères. A fit of depression in a bar in Reykjavik rather than the geysers on the tundra. Nothing of a basilica at Mtzketa except a woman who was howling and hugging a pillar because her son was dead. A few streets that Georges Perec wanted me to take pictures of for a book he wanted to write ... Georges is dead and I can't even remember the name of the town.

Saddest of all in the attics of memory are the people one also stores there, people one knew and liked and who have disappeared. So, jumbled together, Nicole Plantade elbows Jean Follain, a counselor at a summer camp next to a writer, a laughing face and a glum face, both now lost in time. Everything we have seen and lived ends up like old letters and old photos, forgotten in a box.

BONN, 25 MAY 1994

The crowd swarms through the international exposition; avenues and alleys are crawling with people who, with people whom; elevated trains thread their way through garishly futuristic buildings blazoned with neon and screaming colors; people shove each other to get a glimpse of the more prestigious exhibitors. This enthusiasm is impressive but have I really traveled around the world to see this?

The first time I visited an exposition ... was a long time ago. We had to travel thirty kilometers to the county seat. A big trip. A big dream. There were only lanes lined with simple wooden booths and yet already it was the apotheosis of technology and plastics. Not yet sophisticated computers nor communications satellites but already gadgets for dicing vegetables, nylon stockings that didn't run (or hardly), and machines which, it was said, could wash dishes. I who address you here, chosen at random in the crowd of 1950, demonstrate that a bakelite squeegee could, with a simple gesture, spread paint so it imitated the grain and knotholes of wood. What a success! What a marvelous invention, since a ten-year-old child could manipulate it without being taught! The spectators watching me were no less surprised and full of admiration than those of today who look at machines that reproduce three-dimensional virtual images or the electric robot that will replace the seeing-eye dog. The commentary will always be the same: It's amazing what they can do these days, time marches on.

In fact, two days later, in a museum, it seems to me that I haven't come to this country to marvel at the advances of technology, but rather to meet a stone personage sculpted at the edge of a large block of limestone. He has been climbing, scaling for centuries and, for centuries, always with that same tactile sensuality that those who have seen him feel from their eyes to the palms of their hands: his rounded forms, the unclenched muscles of his legs, his arms, his back. His face is probably one of the most beautiful in the world, but since his back is turned, we see only his wavy hair. He is completely absorbed by his effort; he is rising.

Instead of advancing, we too ought to try and rise.

TAEJON-KYONGJU, 26 & 28 OCTOBER 1993

The apples we bit into eagerly, without waiting for them to ripen. And the peaches, the apricots, as sweet as the imperceptible down on their cheeks where the fine hair of the temples begins. Whether we succumb to blue moods or paint the town red, the tresses will still end up white, as if the boundaries of everyone's stories are traced especially at the temporal periphery of the body — the hair, the nails, the teeth. When all is said and done it's better to lose oneself in the story and the rest. When all is said and done.

The white-haired gentlemen no longer look so closely at the tresses of their companions of days gone by. Since the time when together they seized the day, the fruit and everything, in handfuls, their look has changed too. Hair can be masked with dye, nails with polish: Are they still as attractive? If the smile remains the same, the teeth, cavities filled, nerves deadened, are no longer set on edge by unripe fruit; but dimples speak tellingly of apples that are getting overripe. The aging gentlemen pay more attention to the legs, for, if cellulite and varicose veins have held off, it's in the legs of the female that time has less to grasp at. To be continued.

(And then in memory, ancient rose, yes, of the time when I entered your history, ill-equipped, and of the faint blue cobwebs one notices in places where the skin is finer, milky way, ill-loved. And all the same, what happiness it was!)

The legs, one ought to look at them with one's own eyes that the flow of years and events haven't misted—a few events then a few more and still more, until it turns into a wave, faster and faster, confusion, vertigo, a cataract. Then one begins looking up from the shoe, the ankle, the calf. Then the swelling of the knee, the more supple curve of the thigh that flees beneath the skirt. And yet one climbs, one continues to climb in time as far as the silky space where the thigh is cut off by the panty. But that's enough. One stops, fearful that the fingers will tremble with more than the tremors of Parkinson's. If the hands aren't sick, there are still the fingertip variations of the warmth, let's say, the velvetiness, the suppleness of the skin or is it merely variations of memory that deludes itself with its intermittences, its failures. The machine is straining now, as though fearful of running out of gas at the bend in the highway. To be continued. Up until the moment when the fingers of memory grasp nothing but emptiness, the fear that can't be shared, the last. End of the comedy, there's nothing more to see.

BONN, 16 MAY 1994

It's raining on the city. The surrounding mountains clutched by office buildings are smoky with vapor. One tells oneself that the rain won't last, that it's only water from a precocious monsoon that slaps one's face; the faint acrid taste on one's lips is due to air pollution, like the water in the hotel swimming pool whose chlorination produces a vague taste of menthol.

Denaturation isn't the prerogative of modern times. Even grenadine, the drink of days gone by, was no less artificially colored and only the insouciance of youth made it taste good. Without saying a word to one's parents or the rest of the gang, we sped off into town on our bikes, we strolled happily in the public garden before swilling for an hour a *menthe à l'eau* of the most gorgeous chemical chromaticism, all the while talking about the weather and school where they still taught you to memorize—"*Rodrique, qui l'eût cru*"*—then, on the way back, the sun in a few kilo-

---

* TRANSLATOR'S NOTE: from Corneille's *Le Cid*.

meters dried blouse and sports shirt made of the first nylon fabrics; and we returned home with all that adventure in the secrecy of ourselves.

Cool water, spring water, rain water, bad weather polish the ridges of the cliffs, bleach the colors, dig the trenches in the wild meadows, and the acid dejecta of industry, the salt of tears impregnate nature. Cute little faces, pretty faces, bloated faces and mugs are faded. Whether clothed in natural silk or synthetic fabric, the body changes with the landscape: male paunches swollen with too-rich food, female thighs wavy with cellulite, the heart becomes an inert stone, the vaginal shelter a smooth, dry sac. Natural and artificial aren't the cause. It's life and in every case it's not the little death that makes us shudder at the end.

So be it, it's understood. Okay, okay. But meanwhile: Every cloud has a silver lining: it's a matter of drinking it all up to the last drop and adding as little water as possible to the wine; let's fill our glasses and renew our vows: Here's to you, old pal. What's natural is the pleasure we take in living in spite of everything, with everything, and even with wine that's just a little adulterated with chemicals, with more or less artificial water. The rain has a different taste but it's still rain; people change their tastes too and they continue to live.

HOTEL OLYMPIA, SEOUL, 6 FEBRUARY 1993

FROM

DEMONSTRATIONS AND FABULATIONS

TRANSLATED BY JOHN ASHBERY

Her eyes shut, her teeth clenched, tossing her head violently from side to side, she was moaning as though suffering greatly. Then she arched her back with so much force she raised him up. It was at that moment of their little death that he heard the familiar sound of the train in the distance, but as though the pulsing of the wheels against the rails was just under their entwined bodies. The next instant, fallen on her again and with his face buried in her hair between her shoulder and her neck, listening to their two hearts knocking like a fist against a closed door, he suddenly remembered two lines of an old poem: But always at my back I hear / Time's winged chariot hurrying near. Her eyes must have been open by then, beautiful and gleaming, gazing into emptiness, gone in the thoughts he knew nothing of.

Despite the system of dual keys and the electronic surveillance, they succeeded in getting into the lobby of the building. It took them then about fifteen or twenty minutes to destroy everything. It's true: everything that could be trashed: the walls were smeared with spray paint, the plants ripped out, trampled on, the windows smashed, the seats slashed; the floor was littered with beer cans; there were two syringes and even urine. Those tenants who heard the uproar were careful not to leave their apartments. From behind their armored doors they called the police, as in olden times the lord of the castle would unleash his troops against a band of highwaymen. But when the police arrived, the gang had already fallen back into the no man's land of the streets.

Animals mark off their own territory, but those poor hordes of men teeming with dull rage can barely mark their own passing, with pillaging signed with initials and tags copied from comic strips: Rascals, Bozos, Wow, Killer, in ornate lettering as primitive as their gear of chains, death's heads and swastikas. And I was saying that they reject society because it has rejected them.

It's easy to talk that way, Bill replied, as long as it's not one of your friends who's been stabbed by someone looking for money for a fix and because it's not your wife who has to pass them every day in the street where anything can happen.

Yes, it is easy. I'm in a hurry perhaps to exhibit my understanding while there's still time, before a too-close shave plunges me into the dark Middle Ages.

NEW YORK

Serge Fauchereau was born in Rochefort, France, in 1939. After teaching at SUNY Stony Brook and the University of Texas, Austin, he worked for the Centre Pompidou for 11 Years. During that time he curated exhibitions such as *Paris-New York* (1977), *Paris-Berlin* (1978), *Paris-Moscow* (1979) and *Paris X 4* (1986). A contributor to numerous catalogues and publications, he is the author of over thirty books (fiction and essays), most of which have been widely translated. In America, translations of Fauchereau's essays on art include: *Braque* (Rizzoli, 1987), *Arp* (Rizzoli, 1988), *Kupka* (Rizzoli, 1988), *Malevich* (Rizzoli (1992), *Mondrian* (Rizzoli, 1995), and *Moscow 1900–1930* (Doubleday, 1993). Since 1994, he has been the artistic consultant of the European Parliament, Espace Léopold, in Brussels. Currently, he is a curator for the Museo Nacional Centro de Arte Reina Sofia, Madrid.

BLACK SQUARE EDITIONS   EDITED BY JOHN YAU

*The Footprints of One
   Who Has Not Stepped Forth*
RICHARD ANDERS

Drawings
EVE ASCHHEIM

The Garrett Caples Reader
GARRETT CAPLES

Simply Separate People
LYNN CRAWFORD

Giacometti: Three Essays
JACQUES DUPIN

Dark Property
BRIAN EVENSON

Complete Fiction
SERGE FAUCHEREAU

*Painting
The Paradoxes of Robert Ryman*
JEAN FRÉMON

*Extracts from the Life of a Beetle
The Recitation of Forgetting*
FRANCK ANDRÉ JAMME

Fathom
ANDREW JORON

me With Animal Towering
ALBERT MOBILIO

Bayart
PASCALLE MONNIER

Ecstasy Shield
CHRISTOPHER NEALON

Echo Regime
JOHN OLSON